A GOLD STAR FOR ZOG

By Julia Donaldson

Illustrated by Axel Scheffler

Arthur A. Levine Books
An Imprint of Scholastic Inc.

Madam Dragon ran a school, many moons ago.
She taught young dragons all the things that dragons need to know.

Zog, the biggest dragon, was the keenest one by far.
He tried his hardest every day to win a golden star.

All the dragons in Year One were learning how to fly.
"High!" said Madam Dragon. "Way up in the sky!

"Now that you've been shown, you can practice on your own
And you'll all be expert fliers by the time you're fully grown."

Zog went off to practice,
flying fast and free.

He soared and swooped
and looped the loop . . .

then crashed into a tree.

Just then, a little girl came by. "Oh, please don't cry," she said.
"Perhaps you'd like a nice sticky Band-Aid for your head?"

"What a good idea!" said Zog. Then up and off he flew,
His Band-Aid gleaming pinkly as he zigzagged through the blue.

A year went by, and in Year Two the dragons learned to roar.
"More!" said Madam Dragon. "Louder, I implore!
Now that you've been shown, you can practice on your own
And you'll all be champion roarers by the time you're fully grown."

Zog went off to practice.

He roared with fearsome force.

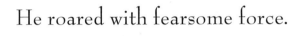

He kept it up for hours on end . . .

but then his throat grew hoarse.

Just then the girl came by again. She said, "What rotten luck!
Perhaps you'd like a nice soothing peppermint to suck?"

"What a good idea!" said Zog. Then up and off he flew,
And breathing fumes of peppermint he zigzagged through the blue.

A year went by, and in Year Three the dragons learned to blow.
"No!" said Madam Dragon. "Breathe out fire, not snow!
Now that you've been shown, you can practice on your own
And you'll all be breathing bonfires by the time you're fully grown."

Zog went off to practice.

He blew with all his might.

He twirled around in triumph . . .

and his wing tip caught alight.

Just then the girl came by again. She said, "You poor old thing. Perhaps you'd like a nice stretchy bandage for your wing?"

"What a good idea!" said Zog. Then up and off he flew,
His bandage flapping wildly as he zigzagged through the blue.

All the Year Four dragons were learning — can you guess?
"Yes!" said Madam Dragon. "How to capture a princess!

"Now that you've been shown, you can practice on your own.
You'll need to capture hundreds by the time you're fully grown."

Zog went off to practice.
He tried and tried and tried,
But he simply couldn't manage.
"I'm no good at this," he cried.

"I'll *never* win a golden star!"
      Just then he saw the girl.
"Perhaps," she said, "you'd like to capture *me*?
      I'm Princess Pearl."

"What a good idea!" said Zog.
      Then up and off they flew,
The princess gripping tightly
      as they zigzagged through the blue.

"Ah," said Madam Dragon. "Our first princess so far!
Congratulations, Zog, my dear; you've won a golden star!"

Zog was proud and happy,
and Pearl felt good as well.

She took the dragons' temperatures,

and nursed them when they fell.

A year went by and, in Year Five, the dragons learned to fight.

"Right!" said Madam Dragon. "Here comes a real live knight!"

Up spoke the knight: "My name," he said,
"is Gadabout the Great.
I've come to rescue Princess Pearl.
I hope I'm not too late."

Zog breathed fire and beat his wings. "You can't! She's mine!" he roared.
"Oh, no, she's not!" yelled Gadabout, and waved his trusty sword.

The other dragons crowded round and watched them, all agog.
Who was going to win the fight, Sir Gadabout or Zog?

Then Princess Pearl stepped forward, crying, "STOP, you silly chumps!
The world's already far too full of cuts and burns and bumps.
Don't rescue me! I won't go back to being a princess
And prancing round the palace in a silly frilly dress.

"I want to be a doctor, and travel here and there,
Listening to people's chests and giving them my care."

"Me too!" exclaimed the knight, and took his helmet off his head.
"I'd rather wear a nice twisty stethoscope," he said.

"Perhaps, Princess, you'll train me up?" And Pearl replied, "Of course,
But I don't see how the two of us could fit upon your horse."

Then Zog said, "Flying doctors! I'd love to join the crew.
If you'll let me be your ambulance, then I can carry you."
"Bravo!" said Madam Dragon. "An excellent career!"
And all the Year Five dragons gave a loud resounding cheer.

Then Madam Dragon told the horse, "I really hope you'll stay.
I'll let you be my pupils' pet, and feed you lots of hay."

"What a good idea!" said Zog. Then up and off he flew,
The Flying Doctors waving as they zigzagged through the blue.

For my first grandchild to be — J.D.
For Gabriel and Raphael — A.S.

All rights reserved. Published by Arthur A. Levine Books, an imprint of Scholastic Inc., *Publishers since 1920*, by arrangement with Scholastic Children's Books, London, United Kingdom. SCHOLASTIC, the LANTERN LOGO, and associated logos are trademarks and/or registered trademarks of Scholastic Inc.

Library of Congress Cataloging-in-Publication Data
Donaldson, Julia.
A gold star for Zog / by Julia Donaldson ; illustrated by Axel Scheffler. — 1st American ed.   p. cm.
Summary: Each year, as Zog practices new skills learned at Madam Dragon's school, a little girl helps him out until one day he finds a way to help make her dream come true for herself, a new friend, and Zog.
ISBN 978-0-545-41724-2 (hardcover : alk. paper) [1. Stories in rhyme. 2. Dragons—Fiction. 3. Schools—Fiction. 4. Princesses—Fiction. 5. Knights and knighthood—Fiction.]
I. Scheffler, Axel, ill. II. Title. PZ8.3.D7235Gol 2012   [E] —dc23   2011026921

10 9 8   18 19
Printed in Malaysia
First American edition, July 2012